Jake Jones v Vlad the Bad

Joanna Nadin ✳ Jonathan Edwards

OXFORD
UNIVERSITY PRESS

Name	Jake Jones
Age	8 and a half
Job	Saving the world
Special weapons	Super intelligence
Villains captured	• Deadeye Dick, one-eyed terror of the High Seas • Mojo Mac, world's maddest monkey • Horseface Harriet, horror of hairdressers
Address	43 Wilton Way, Whereville
Family	Mrs Jones (mother). 35. Mobile dog groomer. Amateur line dancer. Risk factor – low. Mr Jones (father). 36. Works in office doing something with photocopiers. Risk factor – low. Violet Vera Jones (sister and all-round pest). 11. Three times winner of the Bernard Goggins School debating prize. Risk factor – high.

SpyCorps Agent Profile

Jake Jones

Name	Vladimir Badanovski, aka Vlad the Bad
Age	Unknown
Job	Mad scientist and arch villain
Distinguishing features	• Long, waxed moustache • Platform shoes • White lab coat
Special weapons	Cherry-flavoured stun serum; exploding bananas.
Address	Unknown
Family	None. Rumoured to have been raised by eels.
Wanted for	Crimes too evil to list.

Chapter 1 – Jake Jones: Special Agent

Jake was eating the last spoonful of his Chocolate Crispy Flakes when his watch started beeping. Well, not beeping exactly. It was more like playing a tune at double speed while a bright red light flashed.

This would have been fine if Jake had been a normal eight-year-old, and if his watch had been just a watch. But he wasn't and it wasn't. Jake was actually Jake Jones, SpyCorps' youngest special agent. His watch was actually a secret radar transmitter. That noisy tune meant that a message was coming in from HQ. Jake had to do something – fast. But first, he had to deal with Violet.

IMPORTANT MESSAGE!

"What's that?" demanded his sister.

"Er, nothing," said Jake. "My watch alarm." Which was true. Sort of.

"Let me see," said Violet, grabbing his wrist.

"Mum, why has Jake got a watch? I haven't got a watch!" she protested.

"It came free with the Crispy Flakes," said Jake.

"Like that radio that could translate Russian?" said Mr Jones.

"Er, yeah," said Jake, switching the signal off quickly and heading for the door.

"Where are you going?" said Mrs Jones.

"Bathroom," said Jake.

"No he's not, Mum!" yelled Violet. "He's sending signals to mysterious overlords. I've seen it on that spy-film Jake keeps watching!"

"That's nice," said Mr Jones.

"Put the seat down when you're done," said Mrs Jones.

Chapter 2 – Mission impossible?

In the bathroom, Jake flipped a switch on the medicine cabinet. The face of SpyCorps' Chief Controller, Harry Handsome, appeared in the mirror. He looked worried.

"Jake, we need you now."

"What's up, boss?" asked Jake.

"Ever heard of Vince Van Spangle?"

"Sure have," Jake sighed. He was Violet's favourite pop star. He had long, blonde, curly hair and wore tight, silver suits. Jake detested him.

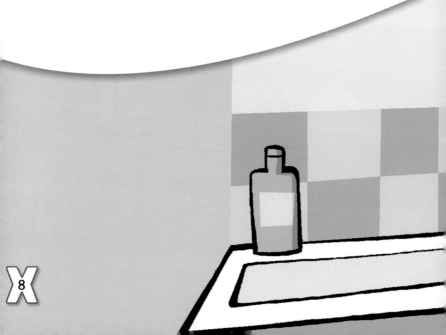

"Well, he's gone."

"Gone where?"

"Disappeared. Kaput. Blammo. One minute he's singing about puppies and chocolate. The next he's vanished into thin air."

"Gosh!" said Jake.

"That's not all," said Harry. "The city's entire supply of vanilla ice cream has gone too."

Vanilla ice cream? Now there *was* something to worry about!

"Are you thinking what I'm thinking?" said Jake.

"I don't know," said Harry, who wasn't as smart as the Chief Controller of a super spy organization should be. "I'm thinking why vanilla? Why not chocolate? Or that one with raspberry ripples in?"

NO
VANILLA
ICE-CREAM

"Because," said Jake, "they don't begin with the letter V. Which means this can only be the work of one man. My arch enemy … " he paused for effect, "**Vlad the Bad**."

"Great Scott!" cried Harry. "Well, there's no time to lose. We don't want any more V words to disappear … except perhaps vegetables. I'm not too fond of broccoli."

"I'm on the case," said Jake. Then he switched the medicine cabinet off.

"What are you doing in there?" demanded Violet. "You have to help. Something terrible has happened. It's Vince Van Spangle," she wailed. "He's gone missing!"

Jake opened the door and smiled. "You don't say."

Chapter 3 – V is for Vlad and Villain and ...

Jake sat at his desk with the dictionary open at the letter V. The trick was to work out where Vlad the Bad would strike next. Then Jake could catch him in the act. Velociraptors, he pondered. Well, they're extinct anyway. Vikings? Ditto. Vowels? Now that *would* be terrible, he thought. There would be no cats, just 'cts'. And no sweets, just 'swts'.

Cheese would be 'chs', but so would choose. And 'bts' could be boots or bits or bats or even bites. And if verbs disappeared that would be even worse. No one would be able to do anything. No walking or riding or eating or climbing … or spying. Jake shuddered. But, making vowels or verbs disappear, well, that would be impossible.

Jake continued to ponder … No, it would have to be something solid. Something real. Something like … Jake scanned the pages. Volleyball? Wrong season. Volcanoes? None of those round here. Voting? No. Vulcanized rubber? No. Vultures … ? Hang on.

15

The zoo had a vulture enclosure! Jake remembered seeing the huge birds looking sullen as they waited for their meal of dead animals. That was where Vlad the Bad would head next. Jake was sure of it.

Jake ran downstairs. He was just about to leg it out the door when Violet blocked his path.

"Where are you going?" she demanded.

"The zoo," said Jake. (He didn't like to lie.)

"Mum!" she yelled. "Jake's going to the zoo on his own."

"Have a nice time," came the voice from the kitchen.

"Ha!" said Jake.

But Violet was not going to be defeated. "I'm coming too."

"Oh really?" said Jake. "But, hang on, isn't that Vince Van Spangle I can see on that motorbike down there?" (There were times, though, when lying was just part of the job.)

17

"Where?" Violet sprinted to the window. At the same time, Jake ran into the hall and jumped into the waste chute. Not your usual exit route, but then this was no usual waste chute. In fact it led to Jake's SpyPortal. There his SpyScooter, complete with invisibility shield and voice command satnav was waiting for him.

Jake slid down the metal tube, making sure he turned left, not right at the third floor. He didn't want to end up in the next-door neighbour's pizza again. At last, he shot out of the end, landed on the SpyScooter and zoomed straight out of the basement door.

"To the zoo!" he commanded. The SpyScooter obeyed.

To the zoo!

Chapter 4 – Following the trail

But he was too late. By the time he got to the zoo, Vlad had already done his worst. Mr Oats, the zookeeper, was in a terrible state.

"I don't understand it," he sobbed. "I'd just given them half a donkey for lunch. They were really excited. Then I went to fetch the ravens for their dessert and, when I got back, they were all gone. Nothing left."

"Nothing?"

"Nothing. Not a feather or a claw. I loved them, those ugly brutes." He threw his arms around Jake.

"Don't worry," Jake assured Mr Oats. "I'm sure they haven't gone far."

"But there's more," wailed the zookeeper.

"More?" asked Jake.

"The vinegar flies and vervet monkeys. They've disappeared too."

"Did you see anyone suspicious?" Jake asked.

"No one," said Mr Oats. "Well, not unless you count that short fellow in the white coat. The one with the funny accent and moustache and giant silver water-pistol thing."

"Vlad the Bad!" said Jake. His theory was right. Vlad was getting rid of everything beginning with the letter V. But how? And why?

"Vlad the Who?" asked Mr Oats.

"Doesn't matter," said Jake. He didn't need anyone getting in the way of business. "Do you know where he went?"

"Well, he asked for directions to the museum."

Ah ha! The ancient Viennese vases! It wasn't strictly in dictionary order but then Vlad was never one for rules.

VERVET
MONKEY

"Thanks, Mr Oats," said Jake. "And don't worry, the vultures will be back."

"I hope so, son. It's really lonely without them. Though I won't miss the flies. Dreadful smell. And the monkeys were no better."

Jake smiled, but there was no time for chitchat. There was work to be done. "To the museum!" he commanded his SpyScooter.

The scene was the same at the museum. The vases were gone and the curator was in a complete flap.

"It's not just the Viennese vases," Mrs Moss cried. "It's also the priceless statue of Venus. And one of the cleaners."

"What's her name?" asked Jake.

"Valentine," sobbed Mrs Moss. "Valentine Vespa."

Jake was stumped. What Vs were left? There were no vestibules he could think of. Mount Vesuvius was in another country. Video recorders? Well, no one used them any more. Then Jake had a horrible thought. A squirmy, scary thought. There *was* another V. It was a colour. And the name of a flower. And the name of his very own big sister … Violet! Jake just hoped he wasn't too late.

Chapter 5 – Vlad the Bad drops by

Jake dropped the scooter off in the SpyPortal and ran up the stairs. (Not even a secret agent can climb *up* a waste chute.) He flung open the front door and ran into the kitchen, where his mum was pouring tea.

"Where's Violet?" he asked his mum.

"She's not home yet. Now, can you go and pick up that invisible ink kit off the hall floor? I don't want our guest to trip up on it. Honestly, all that spy rubbish. I don't know why you bother."

Jake's heart pounded. "What guest?"

"Well, there's a man in the living room. He's from the Vince Van Spangle fan club. He's come to ask for Violet's help in tracking him down. Friendly guy. Very nice moustache. I might get your dad to grow one just like it."

But Jake wasn't listening. In fact, he wasn't even in the kitchen any more. He was already opening the door to the living room.

There, on the sofa, eating chocolate cake, was Vlad the Bad.

"You!" Jake screamed.

"Yes, it is I," smiled Vlad. "Or it was the last time I checked."

"Stay away from my sister."

"Or what?" said Vlad. "You'll zap me with your plastic laser? Or maybe terrify me with your wooden pirate sword? Run away, little boy. I have work to do."

"You touch a hair on her head and I'll … Oh, hello, Mum."

"What are you doing in here, Jake? I asked you to pick up that ink thingy."

Jake thought fast. "I'm helping with the Vince Van Spangle enquiry."

"You don't even like Vince Van Spangle," said his mum.

"I do."

"You don't."

"I do."

"No you don't. You said he sounded like a strangled cat."

Jake had had enough of this. There was only one thing for it. He pulled out his matter-freezing gel pen and zapped her. She froze, her mouth gaping open mid-sentence.

"So, it *is* you," said Vlad, "the famous Jake Jones. The world's youngest secret agent. Lucky I'm wearing a matter-freezing gel pen deactivator."

Jake glared.

"I admire your work," said Vlad, "the way you dealt with Horseface Harriet was really something. But it's all over now."

"Is it?" asked Jake.

"Oh yes. In just a few seconds I will zap you and your vile, V-beginning sister with my dried dog-treat transformer."

"Dried dog-treat transformer?"

"Yes," Vlad said. And he patted a huge, silver weapon strapped around his shoulders. "I invented it myself. It transforms its victims into dried dog-treats. Which I can then feed to my chihuahua, Paris. See these?" He held up a bag of round, brown bits.

"Don't tell me," said Jake. "The vultures and vervet monkeys and vanilla ice cream … "

"And the vinegar flies and Viennese vases and Valentine Vespa," continued Vlad the Bad. "Just Violet left, and then I will be the only V left in Whereville. They will have to rewrite the dictionary, with me as the star."

"You're crazy," said Jake.

"Quite probably," replied Vlad. "All we have to do now is wait for Violet."

"Aren't you going to zap me first?"

"Oh no," said Vlad. "I want you to see for yourself how villainous I am. Then, before I turn you into a fish-flavoured chew, you can call that fool Harry Handsome. I want you to tell him that I am the world's greatest evil genius."

And with that, Vlad threw his head back and laughed an evil laugh.

Chapter 6 – Goodbye, Violet?

They did not have to wait long.

"Where have you been?" asked Jake as Violet came into the room.

"At Suzy's, looking at pictures of Vince Van Spangle – not that it's any of your business," she replied. "Why is Mum standing like that?"

"It's his fault," said Jake, pointing at Vlad.

"Who's he?" asked Violet.

"Vladimir Badanovski, chairman of the Vince Van Spangle fan club," said Vlad.

"No you're not," said Violet. "Cherry Maybe is the chairperson. I've got an official membership card signed by her secretary."

"No she's not. I am." Vlad the Bad did not look amused.

"Not."

"Am."

"Not!"

"That's it!" Vlad grabbed Jake's matter-freezing gel pen and zapped Violet. "She is an extremely annoying girl," he said.

"Tell me about it," said Jake. It was true. She *was* annoying. She *was* bossy. She called him names and put make-up on his Hans Hero action figure. Why on earth would he want to save her?

"Say goodbye to big sis," said Vlad. He lifted the dried dog-treat transformer and pointed it directly at Violet. "And hello to Vlad the Bad, the vilest and most victorious villain the world has ever seen." He clicked a red lever into place.

Then again, Jake thought, she was his sister. And his mum would never forgive him. She would go on about it for weeks. She'd probably take all his secret spy stuff, which would damage his ability to save the world.

Vlad started to pull the trigger.

"No!" Jake screamed. Quick as a flash, he threw himself in front of Violet.

"What are you doing?" demanded Vlad the Bad. "You'll get yourself turned into chihuahua chow."

"Try me," said Jake.

"I'll get you both," said Vlad, and pulled the trigger. A beam of red light shot out. But when it hit Jake, it bounced back. Back towards Vlad.

"Aaagh!" he cried. "What have you done?"

"An old trick," smiled Jake. "Reflective force-field generator. Disguised as a pair of underpants. I always wear them when I'm on a mission."

"Help me … " wailed Vlad. But it was too late. Within seconds he had turned into a small, rather smelly dog treat shaped like a chicken.

How appropriate, thought Jake. He scooped Vlad off the floor and popped him in his pocket. Then he picked up the bag of dog treats and took them with him to the bathroom. It was time to call HQ.

Chapter 7 – Super spy, super hero

"That's amazing, Jake," said Harry Handsome. "Now all you need to do is find an antidote to the dog-treat transformer."

"Er, I think I've already cracked that," said Jake. "I accidentally spilt some mouthwash on the dog-treats. The liquid has restored them to their original forms. In fact, if you could send a squad down here pretty soon, that would be great."

"The vultures have eaten too much vanilla ice cream, the vervet monkeys are fighting over the remote control and Vince Van Spangle is doing a duet with Valentine Vespa."

"They're on their way, Jake. And thanks again for saving the day."

"No problem," said Jake. "Any time."

The image in the medicine cabinet faded. Jake looked at himself and sighed. "That was the easy part," he thought. He still had his mum and Violet to unfreeze. And how on earth was he going to explain the mess on the carpet that the vervet monkeys had made? Or the broken Viennese vase on the kitchen table?

"It's a hard life being a spy," he said to himself. "But someone's got to do it."

Mrs Jones collapsed onto the sofa. "I still don't understand how all those flies got in the bathroom," she said. "And what happened to that lovely man with the moustache?"

"No idea," said Jake. "I was busy."

"Doing what?" snapped Violet.

"Oh, just saving you from an evil madman," smiled Jake.

"As if," retorted Violet.

But before Jake could think of a witty reply, his watch began beeping again. Jake glanced down. Then he switched it off. Because this time, it wasn't a vulture in distress, or a missing vegetable. It was just a reminder that the big match was about to start on TV. After all, not even a spy could miss his team in the final.

If only he could work out where the vervet monkeys had left the remote control!

IMPORTANT MESSAGE! BIG MATCH